# New Beginnings

The **My Magical Pony** series:

Other series by Jenny Oldfield:

# New Beginnings

### By Jenny Oldfield

### Illustrated by Gillian Martin

A division of Hachette Children's Books

# Chapter One

"Hey, Krista, where's Woody's bridle?" Holly Owen yelled from the tack room.

Krista was busy mucking out Comanche's stable. "Where it should be – hanging on its hook!" she called back.

"Oops, yeah!" Holly reappeared in the stable yard with the bridle. "Sorry, didn't see it!"

"She should try using her eyes," Alice Henderson popped her head over Comanche's stable door and grinned at Krista.

"When did Holly ever do anything for

herself?" Krista laughed. She forked manure on to the barrow, wheeled it out into the yard then paused for breath. "Phew, there's so much to do before next Saturday – I don't know how we'll fit it all in!"

"OK, what would you like me to do?" Alice asked. "Shall I clean tack?"

"Maybe brush the tack room floor first," Krista suggested. "Look, there's Jo. Let's ask her."

Together Krista and Alice approached the owner of Hartfell Stables. Jo was leading her thoroughbred, Apollo, into his stable for the night. She waved goodbye to Nathan Steele as his dad drove him out of the yard.

"Jo, Alice wants to help us get ready for

## New Beginnings

our Open Day," Krista explained. "She'd like
to know what she can do."

Jo grinned and counted off a list of jobs.
"Rake the surface of the arena, collect winners'
rosettes from the horse shop in town, re-paint
the striped show-jumping poles, print out the
programme for the day ..."

# My Magical Pony

"Whoa!" Alice held up both hands and laughed. "Give me something simple!"

"OK, help Krista with tonight's mucking out," Jo decided, disappearing with Apollo into his stable.

"Cool!" Handing Alice a broom, Krista went back to work. "As soon as we've finished this, we can lead the ponies in from the fields."

The two girls chatted as they scooped and brushed. "One week to go!" Krista sighed. *One week to Hartfell's first ever Open Day.*

"I know, I can't wait." Alice brushed the stable floor clean. "I'm entering Nessie into the Best Groomed Pony competition."

"And I'm putting Shandy in for the Fun Races." Whistling as she wheeled the barrow

down the row of stables, Krista looked ahead. "Shandy loves games of musical saddles and all that kind of stuff."

"Let's hope we get lots of new people coming to see the stables – after all, that's the whole idea." Alice reminded Krista. If visitors came and liked the place, it meant that Jo would get lots of new riders to make the money she needed to keep Hartfell going.

"Yeah, let's hope," Krista agreed. Thinking back, she realised that Jo had been looking worried a lot recently, until the Open Day idea had come up during a discussion with Jo's friend, Rob Buckley.

"Without extra money coming in, it's going

to be very hard to keep the stables going through the winter," Jo had confessed. "The feed for the ponies is getting more and more expensive, not to mention vets' bills and money to pay the farrier."

"What you need is extra publicity," Rob had advised. "You need more people in Whitton to know that this place exists. After all, you're way up here on the moors and people don't even realise you're here."

And that's when the Open Day idea had hit them – barely a week earlier. Plans had gone full steam ahead: Rob had designed and printed leaflets advertising the event, Jo had made up a programme for the day, everyone had pitched in with all the help they could give.

# New Beginnings

And now the Open Day was only seven days away and Hartfell was alive with activity.

"Krista, you deserve a break," Jo told her when she arrived at the stables early the next morning. "Why don't you take Misty out on a quick hack before the others arrive?"

"No, I couldn't ..." Krista began, though she would've loved to say yes. The morning was bright and frosty, and there was a whole world out there: moors, cliffs and the wide open sea.

"Yes, you could!" Jo insisted, getting Misty's saddle and bridle. She brought the strawberry roan pony out of her stable and tacked her up. "Now go!" she ordered Krista.

## My Magical Pony

A big grin broke out on Krista's face. "Hey, thanks!" she murmured, quickly stepping up into the saddle. "I'll only be gone for an hour."

"Chill," Jo told her. "Give Misty some exercise. Don't hurry back."

Krista and Misty took the cliff path. It was still early and there was no one else around.

# New Beginnings

"Sometimes I wish I was a seagull," Krista confided. She watched the grey and white birds soar over the blue sea. "Wouldn't it be great to be able to fly?"

Misty snorted, shook her head and walked steadily on.

"OK, so you're happy being a pony," Krista grinned.

Misty's hooves clipped along the rough sandy track. To either side the long grass was white with frost which sparkled in the sunlight. Ahead, the path wound around a bend and out of sight.

"Shall I tell you a secret?" Krista went on. Her spirits soared as she and her pony took time out. "Sometimes I *can* actually fly!"

# My Magical Pony

Misty gave another short snort and this time a quick toss of her head.

"Well, not me exactly. And yeah, I know, it sounds crazy and I've never told this to anyone else," Krista went on in a soft voice, safe in the knowledge that they were alone on the cliff path. "But around this bend we'll come to a tall rock, and this is my very own magic spot."

Raising her head and flicking her ears forward, Misty picked up speed.

"Shall I tell you why it's magic?" Krista whispered.

The pony ducked her head as if to say, *Yeah, OK, if you must!*

"It's because it's the spot where I always stand when I need to call Shining Star,"

Krista explained. "Star is a secret, so you mustn't tell anyone!"

*As if!* Misty gave another toss of her head.

"He's a magical pony who comes to help people in trouble. He lives in Galishe, which is a place way beyond the moon and stars. It's all white and glittery – a bit like this world when it's covered in frost, like now."

Misty trotted round the bend then stopped at a tall rock beside the track.

"This is it!" Krista leaned forward in the saddle and whispered in her pony's ear. "The thing is, Shining Star has wings and he can fly!"

*Stamp-stamp* went Misty's hooves on the frosty ground.

"He flies me everywhere we need to go,"

15

Krista murmured. "We fly over the sea, across mountains – all over the place!"

Misty took a deep breath and gazed up the moor towards the rocky horizon.

For a while Krista was silent. "Did I mention that Star is pure white?" she added at last. "He breathes out clouds of glittering silver dust and trails it

## New Beginnings

through the sky wherever he goes!"

The little roan pony listened and watched.

"Shining Star won't come right now, if that's what you're hoping," Krista explained. She shortened the reins and guided Misty with her legs. "He only comes when there's trouble, and at the moment everything's OK."

Carefully Misty turned on the narrow track until she faced the way they had come.

"In fact, everything's great!" Krista insisted, giving her pony's sides a gentle squeeze. "We're all going to work hard this week and have a brilliant Open Day next Saturday."

There were stable doors to paint, squeaky hinges to oil, tack to polish. "Come on, Misty, time to go!"

## Chapter Two

"Now, Frankie, this will be your chance to meet new people and make everyone go 'aah!'" Krista told the little chestnut foal.

After she and Misty had got back from their ride, Krista had worked all day in the tack room, making sure that every bit and bridle sparkled. Now she was bringing the six-month-old foal in from his frosty field.

Young Frankie pranced happily by her side.

"You're so cute!" Krista explained. "All you have to do is gaze at the visitors with those big brown eyes and they'll melt! They'll be

signing up for lessons with Jo just so they can come back and take a peek at you!"

Frankie trotted daintily across the stable yard. He high-stepped into his stable, to be greeted by Duchess, his gentle mother.

Krista slid the bolt then leaned on the door. "Duchess, how do you fancy joining in the fun races? Or maybe the musical saddles?"

As she chatted, Jo came into the yard with Apollo. "Hey, Krista, don't you have a home to go to?" she called out cheerily.

Krista grinned back. "How did Apollo do over the jumps?"

"Great. He's in good shape for a demo on Saturday. I mean it, Krista, scoot! Everyone else left half an hour ago. If you don't go now,

you won't get home before dark."

"Mum's coming to pick me up," Krista replied as little Frankie nuzzled at her hand. "You're shivering!" she noticed. "What's wrong, little fellow, are you cold?"

"Yes, the temperature's set to drop well below freezing tonight," Jo told her. "Perhaps we'd better put his rug on."

Quickly Krista nipped into the tack room to find the smallest rug on the rail. As she came out carrying it, she heard a sudden noise round the back of the building. *Weird!* she thought, slinging Frankie's rug over the porch rail and going to investigate.

In the dark shadows at the back of the low, single-storey tack room Krista made out a

# New Beginnings

stack of old jumping-poles and long planks of wood. There was other junk piled up against the building too – an old wheelbarrow, some worn-out brooms, a wooden chair with two broken legs.

"Who's there?" Krista muttered as she heard another noise.

# My Magical Pony

There was silence, except for a light scrape which sounded like two pieces of wood rubbing together.

"I know someone's there!" Krista called out, trying to sound braver than she felt. She took two steps towards the stack of wood.

"Shucks, you caught us!" a sarcastic voice said, and two kids stepped out of the shadows. The boy was about thirteen, with dark hair. The girl beside him was taller, with dark red streaks in her mousy-coloured spiky hair and the glint of a row of ear studs to either side of her pale face.

"It's a fair cop!" the girl sneered.

"What are you doing here?" Krista frowned, glad that Jo had come to find her.

# New Beginnings

"What's up?" Jo asked.

"We're collecting wood for the Whitton bonfire," the boy explained, staring defiantly at Jo. "You've got a lot of old junk here. We didn't think you'd mind if we took it."

Jo stared back at him. "I'd rather you asked permission first."

"Yeah well, can we take this wood away for you?" the girl cut in.

"For the November the fifth bonfire?" Jo checked. "It's only October. How come you're so early?"

"Jeez, what is this?" Exasperated, the girl turned away, ready to head off back across the field behind the tack room. "Anyone would think we were trying to break into a bank!"

23

"Yeah, forget it," the boy added. "We don't want your stinking wood anyway!"

That was it – Jo had heard enough. "You're trespassing," she said, running to overtake them with Krista hard on her heels. She faced them, hands on hips.

"Hey, we're going, aren't we?" the girl flung back, trying to sidestep Jo. "See – we're out of here!"

Jo took a deep breath, glaring at the two intruders. "You'll leave by the lane like everyone else," she insisted, heading the duo off towards the gate.

"OK, OK, cool it," the boy said. "Come on, Colette, let's do what the lady says. We can still meet the others down by the old bridge."

# New Beginnings

"Thanks for nothing!" the girl sulked at Jo as she followed her mate on to the lane. Soon the two figures merged into the gathering dusk.

Jo folded her arms. "Was I a bit harsh?" she asked Krista as they walked back to the yard.

"No. They didn't have anything to carry wood on, like a cart or a barrow. Maybe they were just hanging round out there because it's warm and dry."

"Yes," Jo nodded. "Anyway, it reminds me that I should get Alan Lewis to bring his tractor and trailer down tomorrow."

"Will he take the wood?" Krista asked, turning to face a glare of headlights in the lane.

Jo nodded. "Yes, and he'll make sure it goes to the official bonfire site. End of story."

## My Magical Pony

"Good idea." The car headlights caught them in its beam – two solitary figures on the lonely lane.

Krista's mum slowed down and leaned out of the window. "Sorry I'm late!" she called. "Hop in, Krista. I've made shepherd's pie for supper and your dad says he's starving. Best be quick, or else he'll eat it all himself!"

# Chapter Three

*On Saturday Comanche can give free rides up and down the lane!* The idea came to Krista as she lay in bed that night. *He'll be great with the little kids – he never spooks at anything.*

Downstairs the phone rang and her dad answered it. The conversation was short and ended suddenly. A minute later, Krista heard the back door slam and the car engine start.

"What happened?" she asked her mum, going downstairs in her pyjamas, rubbing her eyes.

Her mum turned suddenly. "Oh, Krista, I thought you were asleep."

"I was awake, thinking about the Open Day and making plans. Dad left in a hurry. What's up?"

"Nothing," her mum muttered, turning away and shaking her head. "Go back to bed, there's a good girl."

"Who was on the phone?" Krista insisted. She had a fluttery feeling in her stomach – a sixth sense telling her that something really bad had happened. "Was it Jo?"

"Well, actually, yes, it was," her mum sighed. "Listen, you must try not to worry if I tell you the news."

"What news? Is something wrong with one

28

of the ponies?" Fear shot through Krista like an arrow. "Is someone sick?"

Her mum shook her head quickly. "No, that's not the problem." She took Krista's hand. "The truth is, Jo rang to tell us that a fire has broken out in the tack room. She called the fire brigade and they're sending an engine over from Netherby as fast as they can, but meanwhile she wanted Dad and Rob Buckley to drive over to Hartfell and help her lead the ponies out of the stables."

"Oh!" Krista's legs went weak and she sat down on the sofa. Then immediately she sprang to her feet again. "Mum, we've got to go too! We have to help rescue Comanche and Misty and all the rest!"

# My Magical Pony

But her mum held her back. "No way, Krista. It's much too dangerous. Let the professionals put the fire out. In the morning we can go and help clean up."

"But Dad's there!" Krista cried. She pictured smoke curling under the stable doors, imagined the ponies breathing it in through their wide nostrils, heard them whinny and clatter

## New Beginnings

their hooves against the walls …

"Dad's a grown-up and he can take care of himself," her mum said gently.

"But Mum …!"

"No!"

"I can't just sit here!"

Holding her hand between hers, Krista's mum restrained her. "I know how you feel, love. But we must stay here and wait for news. There's absolutely nothing else we can do!"

"Poor Woody, poor Shandy, poor Drifter!" One by one Krista went through the ponies of Hartfell. Drifter would be the first to panic, she knew. He would be bashing his hooves against the stable door, trying to break it down.

## My Magical Pony

Steadfast Shandy would stand and wait to be rescued, her ears flicking this way and that.

And what about Woody, Holly Owen's tough little chestnut who had turned out to be such a great jumper? "Does Holly know about the fire?" she asked her mum suddenly.

"No. I'd better ring the Owens," her mum decided. "Krista, I want you to be upstairs and firmly back in bed by the time I've finished making this call!" She got up from the sofa and left the room.

*Now!* Krista said to herself. She hadn't planned it, but she was alone and she seized her chance. *Shining Star, I'm coming to the magic spot. Please be there!*

32

# New Beginnings

\*

The cold wind cut through Krista as she stood in the darkness with the tall rock towering over her.

"Please come!" she begged. "I've never needed you so much. Can you hear me? Shining Star – it's me, Krista!"

From a great way off, Krista's magical pony heard her frightened voice. He saw her small, pale figure standing on the deserted cliff path. There was no moon or stars.

"There's a fire at Hartfell," she wailed. "All the ponies are in danger. They need your help!"

Star rose into the air with a beat of his powerful white wings. His coat sparkled

with silver dust as he flew faster than the speed of light.

"Come soon or it will be too late!" Krista pleaded, staring up at the dark sky. She didn't notice the icy wind driving against her.

"Krista, do not be afraid," Shining Star murmured as he sped towards Earth.

She gazed up and saw the heavy bank of clouds brighten. They were rimmed with silver, gusting towards her from over the dark sea. Then one drifted free and floated gently towards her.

"Do not be afraid," Star repeated, showering silver dust on to Krista's face.

"Oh, thank you!" she sighed. Shining Star had heard her pleas. He was here, and now

34

## New Beginnings

they could fly to Hartfell together and save
those precious lives.

The magical pony hovered above Krista's
head. He appeared out of the silver-rimmed
cloud, his white wings faintly beating, his

white neck arched. His silvery mane flew back from his noble face. "I see the red glow of a fire at Hartfell," he told her calmly. "You must climb on to my back."

Krista needed no second invitation. Quickly she scrambled on to her magical pony's broad white back, and almost before she had time to grasp his mane, he had risen from the ground again and was soaring across the moors towards the stables.

"A pony hates fire worse than flood or earthquake," Star reminded Krista as he flew. "Fire spreads swift as the wind, it is hotter than any sun's rays."

"Please don't!" Krista gasped. Already, in the distance, she could see the fire glowing

on the dark hillside. She could smell the smoke in the air.

"Fear and fire melt together in a horse's heart," Star went on grimly. "You must expect all the ponies to be sorely afraid."

"Quickly, quickly!" she begged, holding tight as Shining Star swooped down towards burning Hartfell.

He landed in the field behind Jo's tack room. Krista slid to the ground and looked up the slope at the flaming timber building. Heat from the fire scorched her face, though they stood fifty metres away.

To one side she made out three cars in the yard and several figures running in all directions, yelling and crying out. Two ponies

charged loose into the field and in the glare from the fire she could make out Comanche's brown and white piebald markings, together with Kiki's light bay coat and dark mane. "Thank heavens!" she gasped, seeing they at least were safe.

"Come! And shield your face!" Shining Star ordered, leading Krista up the hill.

Comanche and Kiki thundered past them with shrill neighs. They galloped into the shadows at the bottom of the field.

"The fire's spreading!" Jo's voice called from the yard. "The wind is pushing it straight towards the stables!"

"Where's the fire brigade?" Rob Buckley yelled. "Call them again, someone! Tell them

# New Beginnings

we need them now, not in five minutes!"

Star turned to Krista. "Are you ready?" he asked.

She nodded, trusting him, yet still afraid of the smoke and the flames.

"Breathe in this silver mist," her magical pony ordered. "It will keep you safe from harm."

And so Krista stood in the midst of his glittering cloud, breathing deeply, feeling the magic coolness enter her lungs, knowing that Shining Star would protect her. As he walked boldly towards the flames, she followed.

There was chaos in the yard. Rob was there with Jo, and Krista's dad had just arrived. They had turned on the long hose and were spraying water at the roaring flames.

# New Beginnings

The roof of the tack room was ablaze.
Hundreds of wisps of straw caught light
and blew in the wind towards the stables,
showering them with bright sparks.

"I can't get close enough to unbolt Apollo's
door!" Jo cried. "The heat's too bad. I can't
make it!"

Star wrapped Krista inside his silver mist,
and, invisible to the others, they stepped
through the furnace to free Jo's beloved
Apollo.

Inside the stable, the terrified thoroughbred
reared and pawed the smoke-filled air. His
eyes rolled, his ears lay flat against his head.

Krista slid the bolt back and the door
swung open. Apollo reared once more then

whirled towards the door. He charged madly through the space, blundering past Krista, fleeing for his life.

"How did he break free?" Jo gasped, seeing only the pale grey shape of Apollo hurtling past.

Krista's dad shook his head and turned the hose on the flames that licked across the space between the blazing tack room and the row of stables. "It's spreading!" he said grimly.

"Come on!" Krista cried to Shining Star. Still she breathed freely inside his glittering cloud.

They ran along the row of stables, swiftly sliding back the bolts and setting the ponies free.

## New Beginnings

First Misty, then Scottie, Woody and Shandy fled from their stables, wild with fright. The yard echoed with the sound of their clattering hooves.

In the distance, a fire engine's siren split the night air.

"At last. Thank goodness!" Krista's dad yelled as they rounded up the ponies and led them safely into the field.

43

# My Magical Pony

"Now there's just one more stable!" Krista muttered to Star as she braved the brightest, fiercest glare from the flames. "Duchess and Frankie are in that corner where the fire is worst!"

Shining Star nodded calmly and led the way.

Flames licked at the edge of the stable door as Krista slid the bolt, Inside, Duchess had pushed her foal into the furthest corner and stood guard, ready to defend him with her life.

"It's OK, we'll get you out!" Krista promised. "Trust us!"

Duchess raised her head and whinnied. Light from the fire glowed red on her chestnut coat. Frankie cowered behind her.

44

Krista held open the door as smoke
billowed in. "Run!" she pleaded. "Quickly,
before it's too late."

At last Duchess saw that she and Frankie
could make a break for it. The mare nudged
him out of the smoke-filled corner. He trod
shakily, trembling from head to foot.

# My Magical Pony

"Run, Frankie!" Krista urged again.

The foal swayed and sank to his knees. His mother nudged him again and forced him to his feet. This time, Frankie lunged towards the door.

"Good!" Krista murmured, praying that, with Duchess's help, Frankie was strong enough to make it.

He tottered forward – one, two, three steps and he was out of the death-trap into the yard with his mother urging him on. At last, Frankie and Duchess were free of the choking smoke and flames.

# Chapter Four

"How did the fire start?" a fire officer asked Jo as his men swiftly quenched the flames.

Safe in the field, the ponies gathered in a huddle by the bottom hedge.

"I can't be sure, but ... well, there *were* a couple of kids hanging round here earlier tonight." With her sleeves rolled up and with streaks of soot and ash on her face and arms, Jo recalled the intruders. "They said they wanted firewood for their bonfire, but I think it was just a new place for them to hang out. I sent them packing."

"So you think they came back to cause trouble?"

From the shadow of the stable block, Krista stood beside her magical pony and listened. *Tell them the girl's name – Colette!* she urged Jo silently.

"I'm sure it wouldn't have been on purpose," Jo answered. "I suppose they might have been messing about with matches and stuff, the way kids do. Perhaps it was a joke that got out of hand."

"Sounds like something the police would be interested in," the fire officer told her. "After all, there's a fair amount of damage here. It'll cost a few thousand pounds to put right."

*And the ponies almost died!* Krista added

48

silently. She felt anger rise inside her.

Jo sighed. "Let me think about it. For the time being I'm just glad that none of the ponies and horses were injured."

The fireman nodded. "Yeah, that was lucky. Who let them out of the stables?"

"I'm not sure. Everything was confused because it was dark and smoky. There were three of us here, running about like maniacs, trying to douse the flames with a single hose."

Silently Krista grinned at Shining Star and slipped an arm around his neck. "Thank you!" she whispered.

The magical pony lowered his head and let her stroke his face.

# My Magical Pony

"OK, lads, the job's done!" The senior fire officer called his men. "Let's pack up and see if we can make a better job of making our way back down the narrow lane in this fire truck than we did coming up the hill!"

Quickly and efficiently the men packed up their gear while Krista and Star crept out of the yard, round the burnt-out shell of the tack room and into the field.

"Climb up!" Shining Star told her. "I will fly you back home before anyone knows you're gone!"

And so Krista and Star rose in the sky as dawn began to break and the wreaths of smoke from the dreadful fire began to lift from the hillside. The sun rose in the

## New Beginnings

east, spreading its deep pink rays.

"'Red sky in the morning' ..." Krista
murmured part of an old rhyme to herself,
suddenly gripped by a sense of fresh unease.

Star beat his wings and skimmed the tops
of trees. He rose higher. "You sound afraid,"
he commented.

# My Magical Pony

"Yeah. 'Red sky at night, shepherd's delight,'" she explained. "'Red sky in the morning, shepherd's warning.' It means today's going to be a bad day if the dawn is this colour."

Shining Star flew on smoothly towards High Point Farm. "Do you believe this saying?" he asked.

Krista shook herself back into the moment, gazing down at the rough moor scattered with dark boulders, dotted with tiny sheep. "No. I think it's more about the weather. And Mum says it's an old wives' tale. After all, we saved the ponies, didn't we?"

"We did," Shining Star agreed, carrying Krista safely back to her bed.

# New Beginnings

*

"Jo's devastated," Krista's dad reported at breakfast, soon after he got back from Hartfell. He was covered in soot and smelt of smoke. "The tack room is burned to the ground – just a few charred stumps left standing."

Krista's mum frowned as she poured tea and made toast. "Did you manage to save any of the tack?"

"Not a single thing. She lost every saddle, every curry comb and brush. There's nothing left."

Krista sat at the kitchen table trying not to cry. But the tears spilled over on to her toast and marmalade. "Mum, can I go and help now?" she begged.

"Soon." Her mum studied her closely. "You look awful, Krista. Are you sure you're OK?"

"I didn't sleep much," Krista confessed, wiping away her tears and putting on a brave face. "But see – I'm fine!"

("You were very brave," Shining Star had told her as the pink sun rose and he said goodbye. "I must return to Galishe now. Remember, say nothing about what we did. Our secret is precious and must not be shared."

## New Beginnings

He'd flown away and left her with an ache in her heart.)

"You don't *look* fine!" her mum said now. "But listen, cheer up. Your dad is convinced that all of Jo's ponies survived the fire. By some miracle they all managed to break out of their stables and run to safety."

"That's right," Krista's dad insisted. "Look on the bright side. OK, so the tack room's wrecked and all the tack is gone, but at least no one got hurt."

"What about Open Day on Saturday?" Krista's mum wanted to know if anyone had considered this. "I expect Jo will have to cancel everything, won't she?"

Krista's dad nodded. "Right. There's no point now, is there?"

"Of course there is!" Krista argued, starting up from the table. "We've got to have the Open Day after all the work everyone's done!"

Her mum and dad stared at her flushed face. "Calm down," her mum said. "Think about it, Krista – Jo won't be in the mood to invite strangers to Hartfell after what's happened."

"But how will she raise money and keep going if she doesn't get new people?" Krista protested. "And she's going to need thousands of pounds more now, what with new saddles to buy and everything!"

Her dad frowned and shook his head.

## New Beginnings

"Yeah, it's a bad situation, I know."

"Jo has to go ahead with the Open Day!" Krista cried. "She has to!"

"Calm down," her mum repeated.

But Krista dashed outside without listening.

So this was what the red sky warning had been about – the day had begun badly with the fire and was rapidly getting worse. "At this rate, Jo will have to close Hartfell," Krista muttered miserably.

She sat on the garden bench watching Spike, her pet hedgehog, waddle across the frosty grass towards her.

"Just because some kids were messing about – now look what happened!"

# My Magical Pony

Spike thrust his pointed black snout into a small pile of leaves trapped under the bench. He made a rustling sound as his whole body disappeared.

"Jo's lost everything!" Krista went on. "OK, so me and Shining Star, we saved the ponies' lives, but what now? If Jo doesn't hold the Open Day and she doesn't get extra money to buy new saddles and stuff, then she'll have to close the stables and then who knows where Kiki and Shandy and all the other ponies will end up?"

## New Beginnings

Spike trudged through the pile and came out the other side with leaves stuck to his spines. He waddled on up the lawn towards his winter nesting-box.

"You think I'm making it sound worse than it is!" Krista sighed when she saw the little hedgehog carry the leaves inside. "But I'm not!"

For a while she sat on the cold bench, staring at the pale blue sky. In her head she went through all the choices, then she took a deep breath and stood up. "OK, so I know what we have to do!" she said, louder than before.

Her mum came out of the house and called her name. "Krista, I'm ready to drive over to Hartfell now, if you still want to come!"

# My Magical Pony

Krista nodded and ran up the slope. "You bet!" she yelled.

She would call Janey, Alice, Nathan and Holly. The kids would join together and work every single second of the day between now and Saturday. They would clear up the mess, paint the stables, groom the ponies, make everything as good as new.

Jo's Open Day would happen in spite of the fire. It would be a success.

"We'll start over!" Krista told her mum as they drove down the winding lane. "We'll do it for Jo and the ponies of Hartfell, you wait and see!"

# Chapter Five

"I'm not sure if we *can* begin all over again."
Jo shook her head sadly.

Krista and Alice had been the first to arrive
and view the scene of devastation in the cold
light of day. Wisps of smoke still rose from
the black ruins of the tack room; flakes of
grey ash blew across the empty yard.

"Yes we can!" Krista insisted. "We've got six
days to clean up and get ready for the visitors.
We can do it!"

"But is it worth it?" Jo sighed. "I've lost all
my tack, remember. How can I teach lessons

and lead treks without saddles and bridles?"

At that moment, Holly drove into the yard with her dad. She jumped from the car and ran towards them. "How's Woody? Is he OK?" she cried, almost falling over herself in her rush to find out.

"All the ponies are fine," Jo told her. "Woody broke free of his stable. He's out in the field along with the others."

Holly closed her eyes tight. "Thank heavens," she muttered, turning to tell her dad.

Mr Owen, dressed in a grey overcoat and grey checked scarf, looked stern as he surveyed the scene. "How did the fire start?" he asked.

"We don't really know," Jo told him in a

flat voice. Her face was pale and dazed.
"I'm afraid Woody's tack was lost, along with
the rest."

Holly's strict dad frowned. "I take it you
were insured?"

Jo nodded. "I'll put in a claim later today,
once the police have been. But I expect the
money will take a while to come through. I
was just saying to Krista and Alice, I simply
don't know how we're going to get through
this disaster."

To everyone's surprise, Mr Owen softened
and took Jo's side. "Don't worry, you're a
tough cookie – a survivor. Knowing you,
you'll soon pick yourself up," he told her.
Then he stood and thought for a moment.

"Listen, I know a big tack supplier in Netherby," he went on. "The owner is a close friend of mine. He's called Clive Derby. Why don't I give him a call?"

"Yeah, Dad!" Holly urged. "See if he can lend Jo some saddles and bridles …"

"… Before Saturday!" Krista cut in. "Tell him we need them for our Open Day!"

Mr Owen nodded. "Maybe Clive will sponsor your event – donate some tack in return for your advertising his shop."

"Cool!" Alice cried, as if the deal was already done.

"I'm not promising anything," Mr Owen cautioned Jo as he walked back to his car. "But let me have a word and see what I can do."

64

# New Beginnings

*

"New beginnings!" Krista's mum exclaimed.
She came out
of Jo's house
with a tray
of drinks and
biscuits for
the willing
helpers.
"Hartfell is
rising from
the ashes –
literally!"
Alice

aimed the hose at
the blackened walls of Comanche's stable.

The filthy water trickled down the walls then Krista and Holly swept it out into the yard and down the nearest drain.

Next door, Nathan Steele and Janey Bellwood emptied sooty straw from Kiki's stable.

"Good job!" Krista's mum told them as she handed out refreshments.

Meanwhile, Jo talked with a police officer about the cause of the blaze. "There were two kids," she told him. "A boy with dark hair. A taller girl with red streaks in her hair and rows of studs in her ears. They mentioned some other friends, but I didn't actually see them."

Carefully the policeman jotted down everything Jo told him. "It's not a lot to

go on," he warned. "But we'll follow this up, don't you worry."

Jo sighed. "The damage is already done," she pointed out.

The policeman tried to cheer her up. "Look at these kids – they're really putting their backs into their work. You must be glad to have them around."

Jo nodded. But her bleak mood wouldn't shift. "They're keen, but they're young," she pointed out. "They can't possibly realise the size of the job they've taken on."

"It's going to be really, really tough!" Krista confided later that day. She stood on the magic spot, hoping that Shining Star would

hear her. "There were five of us cleaning out the stables, working like crazy so that Jo could bring the ponies in from the field before it got dark. We made it, but only just."

Krista recalled how Drifter had dragged on the lead rope as Jo had tried to lead him into his stable.

"He doesn't like the smell of the smoke," Jo had explained. "It's still in the air, even after you've washed and scrubbed everything from top to bottom."

The nervous chestnut had pulled and reared up. He'd almost succeeded in tugging the rope out of Jo's hand, until Krista had tempted him inside with a bucket of feed.

Other ponies had gone in more easily.

68

# New Beginnings

Good old Comanche had simply taken a sniff at his stable door then ambled in. Shandy too had taken the events of the night before in her stride.

"We finished scrubbing then Alan Lewis arrived with a load of fresh straw." Krista wanted to tell her magical pony about their progress. "We all loaded it into barrows and made the ponies comfortable. We did our very best."

Could Shining Star hear her? she wondered. She gazed up at the grey sky, hoping for a sign.

"Alice had to leave early, but she promised to come back tomorrow," Krista went on, sighing as she spoke. Her arms ached from

brushing and scrubbing, lifting and carrying. "Nathan can't come, but Janey and Holly said they'll be there too."

The wind blew in from the sea, bringing a cold mist with it. In Galishe, Star stood in a

silvery pasture studded with small white flowers. He listened quietly.

"The problem is, we haven't even started on the tack room yet," Krista went on. "It's Monday tomorrow. There's a whole heap of burnt wood to clear away, and Jo says we ought to rake through the ashes to see if we can find anything worth rescuing, like metal snaffles for instance."

Shining Star heard what Krista said. He knew it was time to speak. "Do not give in," he said in his wise, slow voice. "You can do this, Krista. Believe me."

She heard a voice sighing in the wind, closed her eyes and saw her magical pony surrounded by silver mist.

"Do not give in," he said again. "Though the task is hard, the reward is great. Have faith."

Krista nodded then opened her eyes. The grey sky was empty. Way below, the waves crashed against the shore.

"Stand clear!" Alan Lewis yelled as he drove his tractor into the yard at Hartfell.

Matt Simons and Rob Buckley followed him up the lane in their Land Rovers.

"What's going on?" Krista cried. She and Jo ran to speak to the young farmer at the head of the procession.

"We've come to help shift the debris," Alan explained, climbing down from his cab.

# New Beginnings

Krista gasped. "Wow, that's cool! But what's all this wood for?" She pointed to the trailer behind the tractor, stacked with thick beams and broad planks.

"For the new tack room," Alan grinned. "When word got round the neighbourhood about the fire, we clubbed together and decided we could knock something together, no problem."

Speechless, Jo stared at the timber.

Krista ran to greet Rob. "Are you serious?" she demanded. "Are you really planning to build us a new tack room?"

Rob nodded. "Alan and Matt are the experts. They've built barns and hen huts before. I'm just the labourer."

# My Magical Pony

"Wow! I mean, wow!" Krista stood back as Matt, Alan and Rob began to unload tools from the back of Rob's car. Shining Star had been right as always – if you believed in something enough, you could make it happen. "How long will it take? Will it be ready by Saturday? What can I do to help?"

"Tell me I'm not dreaming!" Jo cried as her friends cleared the site. She turned to Krista's mum. "Is this really happening?"

Krista's mum nodded. "That's an actual digger taking away the debris. Those are real hammers and nails. Listen!"

Sifting through the black rubbish, Krista and Holly picked out ponies' bits and metal

curry combs. They stored them in a heap in a corner of the yard.

"Yuck!" Holly exclaimed as she poked amongst the ashes. "These plastic bottles melted and got stuck to this comb – look!"

"Watch out, kids!" Matt called as he and Rob carried long ladders on to the site. "Mind your heads!"

# My Magical Pony

"Let's go and talk to the ponies," Holly suggested. "I brought some brushes and combs from my house. We could groom Woody if he'll stand still for five minutes!"

So the girls left the hammering and sawing for a while and walked down to the field, where the ponies trotted up to greet them.

"Hey, Kiki!" Krista murmured, laughing as the bay pony nudged at her pocket, looking for a treat. Then she said hello to Duchess. "Hey, girl, where's little Frankie? Oh yeah, I see him. He's down by the hedge."

Duchess lowered her head and nudged Krista's shoulder. Then she followed close on Krista's heels.

"What is it?" Krista grinned. "I'm busy,

## New Beginnings

Duchess. Look, Holly's bringing Woody for a pamper session."

Soon she was brushing Woody's dusty winter coat and Holly was combing through his tangled mane.

"Did your dad ask his friend about the saddles and bridles?" Krista asked brightly as she paused to pick hairs from the bristles. Everything was going so well – was it too much to hope that Clive Derby would also say yes?

Holly nodded. "Yeah. Sorry, I forgot to mention it."

"You forgot!" Krista gave Holly a shove. "How could you forget something so important?"

# My Magical Pony

"OK, so Dad asked and Mr Derby said yes, fine," Holly laughed. "We can borrow saddles and bridles from him for as long as we need them."

Krista's mouth fell open. "Say that again!"

"We – can – borrow – saddles – and—" Holly repeated slowly.

"Got it!" Krista broke in with an excited whoop.

Woody tossed his head and took a step away.

"Cool it, Krista. It turns out Mr Derby owes Dad a favour or two. It also

## New Beginnings

turns out that I know his daughter, Colette, from way back when we competed against each other at Netherby Show."

The name filtered slowly through the mass of information that Holly was bombarding her with. "Colette?" Krista echoed. "How old is she? What does she look like?"

"She's older than us – probably about thirteen. Last time I saw her she'd stopped riding ponies and turned into a rebel. She'd dyed her hair bright red and had all these studs in her ears ... Krista, where are you going? Come back!"

# Chapter Six

Krista ran from the field, racing to tell Jo what she had discovered. "The girl who set fire to the tack room is Clive Derby's daughter!" she wanted to say. "Holly knows her. She fits the description. Come on, let's call 999!"

But halfway to the yard, Krista hit a snag. *Huh, if we turn Colette Derby over to the police, what'll happen to the saddles Mr Derby is supposed to lend us?*

"He won't give us the stuff if his daughter is arrested!" she muttered out loud.

*But she did it – she set fire to the tack room. The ponies almost died!* Krista reminded herself.

## New Beginnings

"Maybe she didn't. Maybe this is a different Colette."

*With dyed red hair and loads of ear studs? Don't be dumb!*

"OK, so what do I do?"

"Hey, Krista, you know what they say?" Alice called cheerfully as she cycled up the lane.

Krista gritted her teeth and frowned. "No. What?"

"Talking to yourself is the first sign of madness! I just saw Holly. Good news, isn't it?"

"What is?" Blushing, Krista walked on.

"Mr Derby is going to lend us the tack. He'll bring it to Hartfell tomorrow morning. Isn't that totally cool?"

# My Magical Pony

*

It was the hardest problem. Should Krista tell Jo her suspicions, or should she keep quiet?

As the men hammered planks of wood to the tall, sturdy frame, and as the kids got to work in the stables with big brushes and cans of white paint, Krista said nothing.

"We hope to get the roof on by Thursday," Matt promised Jo. "Then the building will be watertight and you can store stuff inside, even if it rains."

"Or snows," Matt added, putting out his hand to catch the tiny white flakes which were drifting down from a heavy grey sky.

Jo stood back to judge the day's progress. "Wonderful!" she said, shaking her head then

# New Beginnings

laughing. "And I just spoke to Clive Derby. Not only will he lend us the tack, he says he wants to get big banners and posters printed to advertise our Open Day. Of course, he'll put his own name on them too."

"Yeah, it makes good business sense for him," Alan pointed out. He came to stand beside Jo. "Well?" he asked as Matt and Rob hammered more planks into place.

"Unbelievable!" she sighed. "Yesterday I thought my life had come crashing down. Today I know I'm the luckiest woman in the world!"

In the floodlights set up by Alan and Rob, Krista painted stable walls until late Tuesday

83

evening. Her dad came and helped for an hour then drove her home. Next morning, she was up at 7.30 and ready to be dropped off at Hartfell once more.

"Good luck!" her dad called, reversing out of the yard and heading for work.

"Hey, Krista!" Jo called as she came out of the house. She had the old spring in her step and was smiling for the first time that week.

*No, I can't say anything to spoil this fresh start!* Krista decided.

"How would you like to lead the ponies out before the guys get here?" Jo set out her first plans for the day. "Start with Drifter and Misty. They spook at the sound of the hammering if they get too close."

## New Beginnings

Krista was happy to oblige. The sound of the ponies' hooves clip-clopping across the yard soothed her and she was able to fix her mind on the job in hand.

"Come on, Apollo," she murmured, coaxing the big grey out of his stable. She'd been working with the horses for almost an hour. Now there were only Apollo, Duchess and Frankie left in their stables.

"Krista, I have to nip into town to drop off this form at the insurers' office!" Jo called as Krista returned one last time. "Can you hold the fort until Rob and co. arrive?"

Nodding, Krista disappeared inside Duchess's stable. She found Frankie still asleep in the straw, his skinny legs folded under him. His mother stood close by.

"Hey, sleepy-head!" Krista murmured. The foal opened his eyes but didn't try to stand, even when Duchess nudged him from behind.

# New Beginnings

"Lazybones!" Krista laughed, deciding to leave him for a few minutes while she went back outside to see whose car had just driven into the yard.

It was a large green van with gold lettering which read "Derby's Horse Shop. Phone Netherby 556253".

Krista's heart skipped a beat. The old problem welled up inside her chest. Should she tell Jo about Colette Derby, or not? Taking a deep breath, she walked towards the van.

"Knock-knock, is anybody home?" a man called as he stepped from the van.

"Jo just went to town," Krista explained. "Did you bring the saddles?"

# My Magical Pony

The man, who was in his twenties, with long hair tied back in a ponytail, nodded. "I'm Adam. Mr Derby's my boss and he sent me with twelve saddles and twelve bridles. He included extra bits, plus a boxful of combs and brushes."

As he opened the back doors of the van, Krista peered inside. "Jo didn't say where we should put them," she told him. "The new tack room's not ready yet so I suppose we'd better stack them in one of the stables for now."

"It's OK, you don't have to lift them yourself," the driver explained as Krista took hold of the first saddle. "The boss press-ganged a helper."

## New Beginnings

As he spoke, a tall, slight figure in a baseball cap stepped down from the passenger seat.

Krista took one sharp look at the girl, then another. Suddenly her heart beat hard and fast.

"Come on, Colette, get a move on," Adam insisted. "Chop-chop!"

*Colette!* But this girl wore the peak of her cap low over her face and there were no studs in her ears. Still Krista couldn't be sure.

# My Magical Pony

"Look, Adam, back off. I didn't want to come in the first place!" the girl muttered, turning her face away from Krista. "If it wasn't for my stupid dad, I wouldn't be here!"

"Nice!" Adam commented, raising his eyebrows at Krista.

*That's the same voice!* Krista realised. *Sulky and defiant, like the girl on Saturday.*

"What are you staring at?" Colette demanded angrily as she brushed past.

Krista spotted a neat row of tiny holes around the rim of Colette's ear. Now she was one hundred per cent sure! "It's you!" she gasped. "You were here last Saturday night!"

Colette waited until Adam had taken a saddle towards the nearest stable. "Not

90

me," she bluffed. "I don't know what you're talking about."

"Yes, it was you!" Krista insisted. "You sneaked back, didn't you? You and your mates were messing around and set fire to the place!"

Quickly Colette lifted a saddle and walked away. "You're nuts!"

But Krista stuck to her guns. "You did! You came back!"

"Leave me alone!" Colette muttered. "It wasn't anything to do with me, honest! And if you tell anyone I was here that night, I'll just say I don't know what you're talking about. No one will believe you. They'll believe *me* – get it?"

Shocked, Krista came to a standstill.

"You started the fire!" she whispered as Adam strode back to the van.

Colette glared at Krista then walked on. "No, I *didn't*! And you'd better get that into your head!" she flung over her shoulder as she disappeared into the stable.

# Chapter Seven

"How could she?" Krista fumed.

Adam and Colette had finished delivering the tack and driven away, leaving Krista staring in disbelief.

"She's got a cheek!" Krista strode back to Duchess's stable. "Can you believe it? Colette comes back here as if nothing has happened, pretending she had zilch to do with the fire!"

Duchess stood with Frankie, who still lay in the straw.

"But I know it was her!" Krista went on angrily. "And she *knows* I know!"

# My Magical Pony

Softly Duchess nudged her foal then looked up at Krista.

Krista frowned deeply. "*Now* what do I do?"

Duchess snickered gently and tossed her head.

"It's like I'm trapped!" Krista exclaimed. "If I tell, we turn Mr Derby against us and our Open Day is ruined. If I keep quiet, those stupid kids get away with almost killing you and Frankie and all the others!"

*Get up, son!* Duchess seemed to say as she went on fussing over Frankie.

"What's going on?" Krista asked, paying attention at last. "Come on, Frankie, it's time to get up!"

## New Beginnings

She crouched beside the foal, who stiffly raised his head but didn't try to stand. Krista noticed that his eyes were dull. "Are you sick?" she murmured.

Frankie's head flopped back down on to the straw. Duchess licked his face, but he didn't respond.

"Oh no!" Krista's hand flew to her mouth as she realised something bad was happening to Frankie. She saw that his breathing was shallow and that there were dark patches of sweat on his neck.

Duchess shuffled her feet restlessly in the deep straw. *Do something!* she begged.

*Poor Frankie!* Krista stood up and gazed down at the limp foal. "Do you need a drink?"

she asked, running from the stable to fetch water. As she filled a bucket, Rob drove into the yard.

Krista breathed a sigh of relief. *Thank heavens – here's someone who can help!* "Frankie's sick!" she yelled. "We have to call the vet!"

Taking a quick look, Rob agreed. "I'll ring John Carter. Let's hope he can get up here right away."

"Drink this!" Krista urged Frankie, placing the bucket beside him. But he was too weak to raise himself. "He can hardly breathe!" she shouted to Rob.

"It's OK, I got through to John. He's driving straight up here. Where's Jo?"

"In town. She'll be back soon, but you

should call her and tell her to hurry." With
Frankie gasping for breath and lying there
helpless, all thoughts of Colette Derby were
wiped from Krista's mind. "Don't worry," she
whispered, softly stroking the foal. "You're
going to be OK!"

Frankie gazed up at her with dull eyes.
Beside him, Duchess's hooves rustled restlessly
in the straw.

# My Magical Pony

At last, after what seemed like an age, John Carter drove up the lane and turned into the yard. He examined Frankie and quickly discovered the problem.

"It looks to me like he breathed in some smoke during Saturday's fire," he told Rob and Krista as he sounded Frankie's side. Then he placed his stethoscope against the foal's chest. "Yep, there's some lung damage and an irregular heartbeat, which is why he's breathless and weak. Also, I'm guessing there's an infection in there too."

Krista bit her lip. "Can you help him to get better?" she asked.

"First off I'll give him a shot of antibiotics to control the infection," John explained.

## New Beginnings

"That should help get a little more oxygen into those damaged lungs."

"Then what?" Rob cut in. He glanced over his shoulder to see Jo arriving.

"Then we wait," the vet said, stuffing his stethoscope into his pocket and opening up a sealed syringe.

"But he will get better in the end, won't he?" Desperately Krista clung to the hope that Frankie would make a full recovery.

John Carter concentrated on giving Frankie the injection. "I can't say for sure," he muttered.

"So what are his chances?" Rob asked as Jo rushed to join them.

Frankie quivered at the sharp needle. Duchess stood close by.

# My Magical Pony

"No better than about fifty-fifty, I'm afraid," the vet said at last. "He could pull through. There again, he might not."

Shaking her head, Krista ran from the stable. She ignored Alan Lewis's car and fled from the yard. Soon she was on the lane, climbing the stile and dashing along the cliff path.

"Please let Frankie get better!" she gasped, racing to reach the magic spot. "I don't care about anything else – the Open Day, the tack room – anything! Only, please, please, don't let Frankie die!"

"Krista, be still," Shining Star said.

He stood on the magic spot, waiting for

her. He soothed her with his
calm, gentle
voice.

"It's all my fault!" she cried, feeling the
silver mist fall on her hands and face. Her
heart felt as if it would burst.

"A foal is sick. How can you be blamed?"

"Because I didn't notice Frankie was ill
until it was almost too late!" she cried.

"Duchess tried to tell me, but I didn't listen."

Star folded his great wings and stepped closer. "It is wrong to blame yourself," he explained. "And it does no good. Think now. What can be done?"

"Nothing!" Krista cried. She thought back over the past few days. "Oh, why didn't we call the police when Colette and her friend first showed up? Why did we let them walk away?"

"Who could know they would return?" the magical pony pointed out. He had flown swiftly to join Krista, and he felt her distress deep down, as if it was his own. "Think, my friend. What is the way ahead?"

# New Beginnings

Krista shook her head and let her tears fall. "I just want Frankie to get better," she cried.

Shining Star's glitter surrounded her. He stood quietly by her side.

Krista looked up through her tears. "You can't help me, can you?" she asked with a quavering voice.

"There is no magic I can use," Star replied. "The foal's future does not lie in our hands."

Krista sighed. "I know it." She paused for a long time. "I have to go," she said at last. "I need to be with Frankie."

"Good," Shining Star said. "You have a loving heart."

Krista turned back along the path. She walked out of the shining silvery cloud.

## My Magical Pony

"Star, can you look ahead and tell me – will Frankie be OK?" she asked, longing for a glimpse of the future.

But when she turned and looked back at the magic spot, Shining Star had risen from the ground and was flying high in the sky, faster than light, more brilliant than the brightest star.

# Chapter Eight

Back at Hartfell, Alan and Matt had joined Rob and begun work on the tack room roof. Jo was with Duchess and Frankie.

"How is he?" Krista asked, looking over the stable door.

"More comfortable than he was," Jo murmured. "He's breathing more easily, but his temperature is still high. John says we have to get him to drink as much as possible."

Nestling deep in his straw bed, Frankie looked up at Krista with sorrowful eyes. His mother watched over him.

"Let me take over," Krista pleaded with Jo. "I can stay with him while you get on with all the stuff for Open Day."

Jo nodded. "OK, Nurse Krista! Give me a shout if you need me."

And so Krista settled in to a day of caring for the sick foal. In the background, the men hammered, calling out and whistling as they worked. Alice and Holly arrived to muck out and carry on with the chores. From time to time one of them would peer in at Frankie.

"How is he?" Holly whispered with a worried frown.

"He's sleeping," Krista reported.

Frankie lay on his side drawing shallow breaths into his damaged lungs. He looked small

and weak beside his sturdy mother.

"It's all Colette's fault!" Krista muttered. "Just you wait until I see her!"

Then Matt came in and crouched beside the sick foal. "I heard what happened," he told Krista. "The poor little chap didn't do anything to deserve this, did he?"

# My Magical Pony

The sight of the big, tough farmer gently stroking Frankie as if he was one of his newborn spring lambs brought a lump to Krista's throat. She took a deep breath then went to fetch fresh water. "Drink this," she pleaded, pushing the bowl close to Frankie's head.

For the first time he had the strength to raise himself until he could take a drink. He sucked noisily at the water then flopped back on to the straw.

"Good!" Krista murmured.

Duchess snickered quietly then licked Frankie's face and neck.

And so the day went slowly on, hour by hour, with Krista carefully watching the

patient's every move, until in the evening John Carter returned.

"Let's listen to his chest," the vet said, taking his stethoscope out of his bag. "Hmm," he murmured, moving the instrument over Frankie's ribs and chest.

"So?" Krista held her breath, waiting for the verdict.

"His lungs are beginning to clear," John said at last. "The fluid caused by the infection is easing, thanks to the antibiotic."

"That's good, isn't it?"

John nodded. "It certainly helps. But what we don't know yet is whether or not the smoke damage will heal." He turned to Krista. "Has he been coughing anything up?"

She shook her head.

"If he does, and there's blood mixed in with the mucus, you must call me right away," the vet explained. "Do you know who's going to be nursing him through the night?"

"I will!" Krista said straight away. "I'll stay with him!"

Now John glanced round at Jo, who had just joined them. "He needs someone with him to keep an eye on things."

"Me!" Krista insisted. "I'm not leaving him until he's better!"

Jo nodded. "We'll ask your Mum and Dad if it's OK. I can fix you up with a camp bed and a nice warm sleeping bag."

## New Beginnings

And so arrangements were made – Krista was to stay the whole night at Frankie's side.

The night was dark and misty. In the stables along the row, the ponies munched steadily at their hay.

# My Magical Pony

Krista lay inside her sleeping bag, gazing out of Frankie's stable at the black sky. She remembered what Shining Star had said – that no magic could help heal the sick foal – but still she wished Star was here, breathing his glittering mist over Frankie, keeping him calm, wishing him well.

It was past midnight. All was quiet. Once in a while, Frankie shifted in his bed and Duchess, who was standing over him, would nudge and soothe him. Outside in the yard a barn owl sat on the new roof of the tack room and hooted eerily through the mist.

Then Krista heard another sound – something scuffling across the field behind the tack room and stumbling against a

metal ladder left by the workmen. She sat up and listened.

Next door, Comanche stirred. Further down the row, Krista heard Apollo snort and look out over his door.

Krista listened hard and heard more noise. This time it sounded like footsteps crossing the yard. Who could it be at this time of night? Was it an animal, or was it human?

"Jo?" Krista called quietly as she slipped out of the sleeping bag and went to the door. "Is that you?"

She was in time to see a torch beam flash against the wall of the tack room then swing round towards the stables. But at the sound of Krista's low call, the light suddenly clicked off.

# My Magical Pony

Alarm shot through Krista's whole body. Her fingers fumbled with the bolt as she went out to investigate. "Who's there?" she hissed.

A slight figure ran across the yard and down the side of the tack room. It was definitely someone Krista's age! The kid stumbled in the dark, crashing against a barrow then falling to the ground.

Krista ran after the intruder. No way was this person about to get away with creeping around Hartfell in the middle of the night! She saw the figure struggle to its feet and set off again.

But Krista was gaining ground, almost within reach as the intruder stumbled on. "No way!" she muttered aloud, catching hold of an

arm and forcing the figure to turn.

"Let go!" a voice hissed.

There was a struggle.
Krista held on
tight. She
grabbed at the
baseball cap
pulled low
over the
girl's face
and tore it
off. "Colette
Derby!"

"Just let
go!" Colette muttered,
wrenching free.

# My Magical Pony

Krista threw herself at Colette and brought her to the ground. She sat astride her enemy. "OK, now tell me what you're up to!"

"Nothing. Let go of me. Are you crazy?"

"Tell me!" Krista insisted, staring down at Colette's pale face.

"Look, I heard about the foal being sick, OK! Holly Owen texted me. I came to see how he was!" Colette tried in vain to roll free.

"Oh yeah!" Krista scoffed. She used all her weight and strength to keep Colette pinned down. "Like you care what happens to Frankie!"

"I do!" Colette cried. "Look, I know you think this is my fault, but I didn't set fire to the place, honest!"

Slowly the words sank in and Krista sat

back on her haunches to let Colette wriggle free. She grabbed the girl's torch from the ground and shone it into her face. "If you didn't, who did?" she asked.

Colette blinked and turned her head away. "I tried to stop it happening, but Richie wouldn't listen. You see, we met the others down by the old bridge."

"Yeah, I remember," Krista muttered.

"Richie said we should come back and get the wood. It was freezing that night and they kept talking about having a fire to warm up by. I said no, the ponies would be spooked all over again and the cops would be called."

Keeping the torch beam steady, Krista tried to decide if Colette was telling the truth.

"Is this for real?" she muttered.

Colette nodded. "Richie just laughed at me and called me chicken. The others were all up for it. They snuck back and I guess they lit a fire and it got out of hand. Well, you know the rest …"

"But you weren't with them?" Krista checked. "You were worried about spooking the ponies?"

"Honest, I was! I love horses! I'd rather die than do anything to hurt them! Why do you think I'm here now?"

"So tell me," Krista said. Through the confusion, she saw one thing clearly – that Colette Derby had risked a lot by coming back to Hartfell.

# New Beginnings

"Because I got the text that Frankie was sick and might not make it through the night," Colette explained. "I didn't know if Holly was telling me the truth. I couldn't bear it! I had to see for myself."

"You care that much about a foal you don't even know?" Krista gasped, leading the way back into the yard.

"I told you – I love ponies and horses more than anything in the world! And I blamed myself," Colette muttered, gripping her hands into tight fists as they approached Frankie's stable. "I should've stopped Richie, but I guess he was right – I was chicken! When I eventually heard about the fire, I didn't even have the nerve to go to the cops."

# My Magical Pony

"Ssh!" Krista warned. She held open the door to reveal Frankie sleeping in the straw. Duchess turned her head to study the newcomer.

## New Beginnings

"Poor little thing!" Colette murmured, closing her eyes and turning away.

"Quiet!" Krista whispered again. "It's OK, he's sleeping peacefully. He's not coughing or struggling for breath any more."

"Is he going to be OK?" Colette's voice wavered.

Krista knelt by Frankie's side. His coat was cool and dry, his breathing was even. "I think he is," she told Colette. "He's a tough little thing. If we can get through the night without anything going wrong, I really believe he's going to make it!"

# Chapter Nine

"Jo, come quick!" First thing next morning, Krista ran to the house and knocked on the door.

Jo opened it, still in her pyjamas, blinking in the grey dawn light. "What is it? What happened to Frankie?" she asked, suddenly alert.

"Come and look!" Krista cried. She dragged Jo across the stable yard in her bare feet. "Frankie is standing up!"

There in the stable, the sick foal was standing knee-deep in straw.

## New Beginnings

"He did it all by himself!" Krista told Jo. "I heard him rustling in his bed and when I opened my eyes, there he was!"

Jo nodded and smiled. "He must be feeling better."

"I know! And look, he's even trying to walk!" With her fingers tightly crossed, Krista watched Frankie take a tottering step towards Duchess. "Oh, well done!" she cried.

As Jo quizzed Krista about how much the patient had drunk and slept, the yard grew busy. First, Alan and Matt arrived with big tubs of wood stain and brushes. Then Clive Derby's man, Adam, drove up with a banner advertising Saturday's big event. "The boss told me to string it up across the entrance,"

he explained, unrolling the giant "Welcome to Hartfell Open Day" sign.

"Hey, Frankie, how do you feel?" Alice asked as she leaned her cycle against the wall and came to look.

"Much better!" Krista reported. She was in the stable, gently brushing the foal's soft coat. Jo was in the house getting dressed.

"Magic!" Alice grinned, singing as she went to lead Comanche out into the field.

*Not this time!* Krista smiled to herself. This time Shining Star had not been able to fly to the rescue – but Frankie had got better thanks to John Carter's medicine and Krista's own careful nursing.

"Hey Krista, how do you like this colour?"

## New Beginnings

Matt called as he began to paint the tack room wall a deep, rich green.

"Cool!" she yelled.

The ponies clip-clopped across the yard on their way to the field – Comanche, Kiki, Shandy and Nessie. Rob arrived in his Land Rover, trailering in a load of hay. Finally, John Carter showed up to check on Frankie.

The vet took one glance and nodded. "It's looking good," he confirmed when he saw Frankie standing next to his mother. He sounded the patient's chest, took his temperature and nodded again. "Definitely on the mend," he reported. "Last night was the peak crisis time and it seems he came through, thanks to you, Krista."

# My Magical Pony

Krista blushed.

"I take it you had a nice quiet night with him?" John inquired.

*Yeah, if you don't count Colette creeping up in the middle of the night, scaring the life out of me and confessing every last detail!*

"So what are you going to do about Richie and the gang?" Krista had demanded after Colette had spilled the beans.

"I'm going to the cops," Colette had replied. "Those kids deserve it, don't they? They could have killed all the ponies."

"Yes!" Krista had agreed. She'd watched Colette stroke Duchess then bend over Frankie and whisper.

"I'm glad I came to visit," she'd murmured.

# New Beginnings

"I'd never have forgiven myself if I hadn't."

And she'd left the stables before dawn, determined to go to the police and tell them exactly what she knew about the night of the fire.

"Well, you certainly make a great veterinary nurse!" John told Krista now. "But then we already know how good you are with these ponies. You have a real talent."

Blushing more deeply, Krista grinned and backed out of Frankie's stable, saying she wanted to help Jo carry the saddles into the brand-new tack room.

"We're almost ready, with one day to spare!" Jo sighed, standing with her hands on her hips and surveying the new tack.

# My Magical Pony

Krista breathed in the smell of new timber and wood stain. "Yeah, there's only four stables still to paint, new shavings for the arena to collect, the field to weed, jumps to set up, fencing to fix, gate hinges to oil …" Quickly Krista ran through the long list.

"Point taken!" Jo grinned. "But hey, Krista, we have a new tack room out of the ashes of the old one."

"A new beginning," Krista agreed. A smile spread slowly across her face as she went to check once more on little Frankie.

All day Friday they worked non-stop. The tack room was finished down to the last lick of stain and the last hook screwed into place

for the bits and bridles. Every pony was brushed and combed in readiness.

"You look so pretty!" Alice cooed at Nessie, standing back to admire her dappled grey pony.

129

"And you're so handsome!" Holly told Woody, whose coat shone like a bright new horse chestnut.

Janey and Nathan groomed Comanche and Shandy until they were both spotless.

"Now, Shandy, no rolling in the straw!" Nathan warned before he packed away the brushes and combs.

"Until tomorrow!" Jo told everyone as the autumn sun went down. She took Krista to one side. "I just wanted to let you know that John's given Frankie the all-clear," she said. "His lungs will soon be as good as new."

Krista took a deep breath then grinned.

"*And!*" Jo went on, raising her eyebrows

and staring at Krista with her direct, open gaze. "The police are talking to some kids about Saturday's fire!"

Krista gasped but said nothing.

"All boys, apparently," Jo went on. "Four of them in total. So it seems the girl who was sneaking around here looking for firewood wasn't part of it."

"Right!" Krista nodded. *Hey, good for you, Colette!* she thought. *You did it. You're not chicken after all!*

"Good job we didn't jump to conclusions," Jo added.

Once more Krista nodded. "Red sky," she pointed out, swiftly changing the subject.

"So?" Jo asked.

# My Magical Pony

"'Red sky at night, shepherd's delight,'" Krista explained.

"Yeah, right, got you," Jo grinned. "It's going to be a good day for our Open Day tomorrow."

"Not just good – it's going to be great!" Krista said, making her way home for a sound night's sleep.

# Chapter Ten

"Up with the lark!" Krista's dad laughed as she zoomed downstairs next morning. "Anyone would think today was special!"

"Da-ad!" Krista sighed. She shoved her feet into her boots and zipped up her fleece.

"Don't tease your daughter!" her mum warned. "She hasn't got time."

"It's Open Day. I can't believe that it's actually here!" Krista paused for breath.

"You've been through a lot this last week," her mum sympathised, giving Krista a quick hug. "And you came through with flying colours."

"We all did," Krista reminded her. "Especially Jo. Now all we need is hundreds of people flocking up to Hartfell to see what we do."

"It's going to be sunny," her dad said, glancing out of the kitchen window.

"Oh-oh, I'm late!" Krista glanced at her watch.

"What do you mean? It's only seven …!" Her dad sidestepped quickly as she dashed for the door.

"I'll go by bike. See you!"

"… o'clock!" her dad added.

Too late – Krista was cycling across the yard, down the lane, heading along the cliff path to Hartfell.

*

# New Beginnings

"Welcome to Hartfell Open Day" read the big sign over the gate.

Bright bunting hung from the brand-new tack room, and the newly painted stables were clean and fresh.

Krista was first to arrive, her heart fluttering with excitement. Comanche leaned over his stable door to greet her.

"Hey!" she murmured, stroking his soft muzzle then laughing as he curled back his top lip to show a big row of yellow teeth. "What are you grinning at?"

"Hi, Krista. Does the arena look OK? Did Rob print off the programmes? Where did I put Apollo's martingale?" Jo flew here and there in a total panic as Alice, Janey, Holly and Nathan showed up.

"Yes, yes, and in the tack room," Krista replied. She and the other kids gave the ponies one last brush before the visitors arrived.

"This is a nice place you have here," a woman told Jo as she and her daughter inspected the spotless yard.

# New Beginnings

Kiki and Drifter looked out over their stable doors. Comanche stood patiently while Krista knelt to oil his hooves.

Visitors were filing in and taking a good look at the ponies before they went off to the arena.

Jo saddled Apollo. "Let's go," she told him, riding into the arena for the show-jumping demo.

Krista heard the gasps and applause as Apollo jumped clear. "You hear that?" she asked Alice, who was busy with Nessie. "That's Apollo showing off for the visitors!"

"OK, your turn!" Alice told Nessie, leading her out for the Best Groomed Pony contest. She was up against Holly and Woody, Janey

and Kiki, and Krista and Comanche.

Proudly the kids paraded in front of the growing crowd. The ponies stood with their heads up and ears pricked, knowing they were on show. Meanwhile, Krista spotted Clive Derby talking to Jo, with Colette nearby.

She gave Colette a grin and a thumbs-up. "Hey!" she greeted her as Holly and Woody won first prize.

"Hey, Krista," Colette replied. "How's Frankie?"

"Better," Krista told her. "Come and see."

As Krista led Comanche back towards the yard, Colette chattered on. "Dad's totally impressed with what Jo's doing here. He wants to put up a big poster for Hartfell in

the shop and says he'll tell people to come here to learn to ride."

"Cool." Krista put a saddle on Comanche, ready for the kiddy rides down the lane.

"And I'm going to start riding again," Colette went on. "I've had it with hanging around with Richie and that bunch of losers. Dad and Jo say I can come here and ride the ponies whenever I want."

Krista smiled. "Really cool," she said. And she meant it. "Ready, Comanche?" she asked.

The sturdy pony trod steadily down the lane with his first passenger – a tiny five-year-old boy with blue eyes and a mop of fair hair. Krista held the lead rope and walked ahead.

"Whoa!" the little boy cried at the end of the lane.

Comanche turned slowly and headed back towards the stables.

"Good boy!" Krista murmured, seeing the queue grow longer. For a whole hour he stepped steadily up and down the lane.

Then Alice took over Krista's job and

# New Beginnings

Krista went to find her mum and dad. They had just arrived and stood in a group with Jo, Clive Derby and Rob.

"Good work, Krista!" Rob said, gazing round at the busy throng of visitors. "In fact, I think we can all give ourselves a big pat on the back!"

"For sure," Krista's dad agreed. "This Open Day is a great success. It's doing for Hartfell exactly what you set out to do."

Just then the chattery twin girls peered over Duchess's door and spotted Frankie. "Aah!" they sighed. "So cute!"

Their cries soon drew others to the stable.

"Aah!" everyone said. "A little chestnut foal. Look at his white legs and big brown eyes. How sweet!"

# My Magical Pony

Krista took a deep breath then let it out slowly. *Yes, Frankie, we made it!* Slowly she turned and walked away from the bustle and the noise.

"Krista, where are you going?" her mum called after her.

"I'm taking a break – won't be long," she called back.

And she walked across the lane and over the stile to the cliff path, where the rocks fell away steeply to the beach below.

Krista went slowly, looking up at the moors then out across the silver sea. Soon enough she came to the magic spot.

"Hey, Shining Star," she murmured.

"Hello, Krista," her magical pony replied.

# New Beginnings

He appeared in a bright cloud, his long white mane flowing back from his face, his eyes deep and dark. A silver glow surrounded him.

"We did it," she told him quietly. "We saved Frankie and had our Open Day."

"Then all is well," he said.

Krista nodded.

"And you are happy?" Shining Star asked. He glittered and shone in the bright sunlight.

"Very," she whispered.

"And so am I."

"Thank you – thank you for everything." For braving the flames and the smoke, for shielding her from the choking heat, for freeing the ponies of Hartfell.

## My Magical Pony

"Go now," he told her quietly as he spread his broad wings. "Look forward. Do not look back."

Krista nodded. As her magical pony rose into the blue sky, she walked towards Hartfell and into a shining future.